T0380934

Balboa Press books may be ordered through booksellers or by contacting:

Balboa Press
A Division of Hay House
1663 Liberty Drive
Bloomington, IN 47403
www.balboapress.com
1 (877) 407-4847

The views expressed in this work are solely those of the author and do not necessarily reflect the views of the publisher, and the publisher hereby disclaims any responsibility for them.

Scripture quotations marked NIV are taken from the *Holy Bible, New International Version®. NIV®.* Copyright © 1973, 1978, 1984 by International Bible Society. Used by permission of Zondervan. All rights reserved. [Biblica]

Scripture quotations marked NKJV are taken from the New King James Version. Copyright © 1982 by Thomas Nelson, Inc. Used by permission. All rights reserved.

ISBN: 978-1-9822-2198-0 (sc)
ISBN: 978-1-9822-2199-7 (e)

Library of Congress Control Number: 2019901821

Print information available on the last page.

Balboa Press rev. date: 02/19/2019

BALBOA
PRESS
A DIVISION OF HAY HOUSE

SPECKLE

A JOURNEY OF SELF-DISCOVERY

"Everything is possible for one who believes."

Mark 9:23 NIV

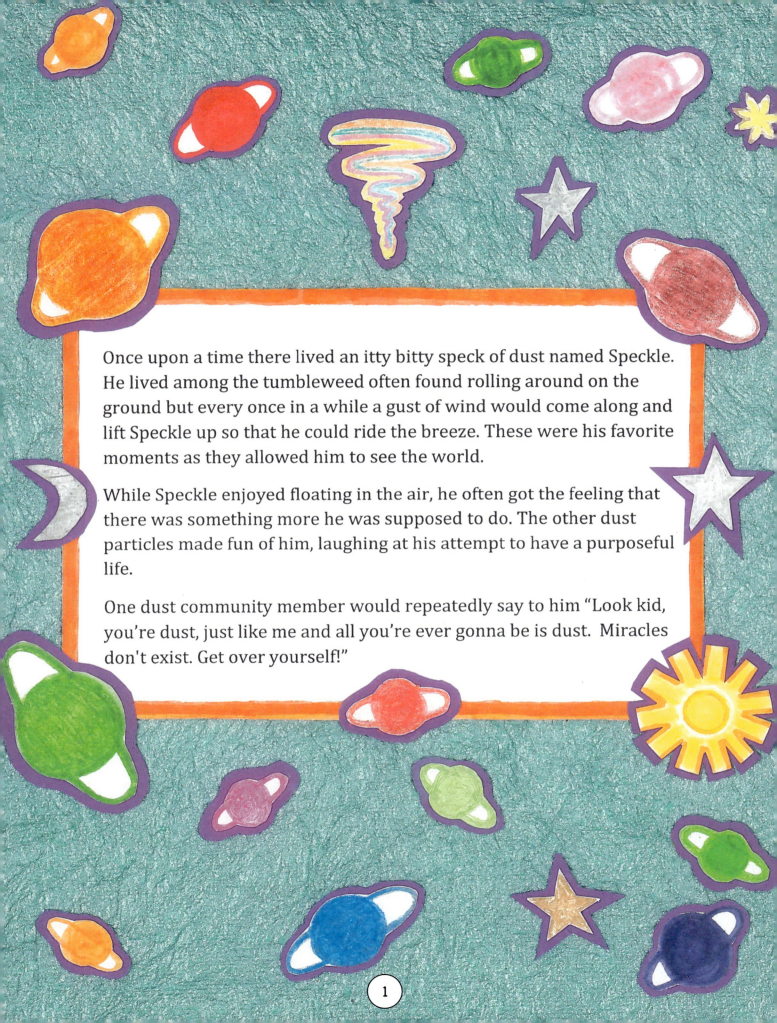

Once upon a time there lived an itty bitty speck of dust named Speckle. He lived among the tumbleweed often found rolling around on the ground but every once in a while a gust of wind would come along and lift Speckle up so that he could ride the breeze. These were his favorite moments as they allowed him to see the world.

While Speckle enjoyed floating in the air, he often got the feeling that there was something more he was supposed to do. The other dust particles made fun of him, laughing at his attempt to have a purposeful life.

One dust community member would repeatedly say to him "Look kid, you're dust, just like me and all you're ever gonna be is dust. Miracles don't exist. Get over yourself!"

Speckle would hear comments such as these and shrug them off. He felt that there was a greater reason for his existence. This feeling would become so strong that he often thought about going on a quest to find meaning to his life.

While drifting one day, he thought to himself, *Look at all of this beauty! There must be something beautiful for me, too!*

Speckle became increasingly curious. He wondered out loud, *"Where did all of this come from?"*

Universe heard him and answered back, "All of this comes from God and God has a plan for every creation."

"Even me? I'm just dust. Does God have a plan for me?"

"Yes, Speckle. God has an awesome plan for you."

"Who is God?" Speckle asked.

"God is ETERNAL and because of God, I exist."

Excited by what he had heard, Speckle asked a bunch of questions: *"Where is God? Where is the plan God made for me? When will I know my purpose?"*

"Soon enough, Speckle, all of your questions will be answered. You'll see…" Universe responded.

Speckle decided he was going to find God. He remembered what Universe said … "God has an awesome plan for you…"

He was excited because for the first time he knew beyond the shadow of a doubt that he too had a purpose. He set out for his mission while saying, *"The God who made the world I see most **surely** has a plan for me!"*

Speckle entered an area full of plant life. He noticed a wonderful scent and realized that the aroma was coming from Flower, who was close by. She was purple, pink and yellow with pretty leaves and a long green stem.

"You're so pretty" Speckle said to Flower, *"and you smell amazing."*

"Why, thank you!" Flower replied.

Speckle felt inspired to ask... *"Flower, do you know God?"*

"Yes, God is BEAUTIFUL. Because of God, I wear vibrant colors and blossom."

Speckle was quiet for a few seconds, and then said, *"Do you know anything about the plan God made for me?"*

Flower responded:

> "God sees your beauty, you are truly unique.

> You have a sweet heart and a healthy physique."

"I think you made a mistake, Flower. You're the one who is beautiful. Not me."

"If you can see it in me it's because it's in you too, Speckle. Beauty recognizes beauty. We are mirrors for each other."

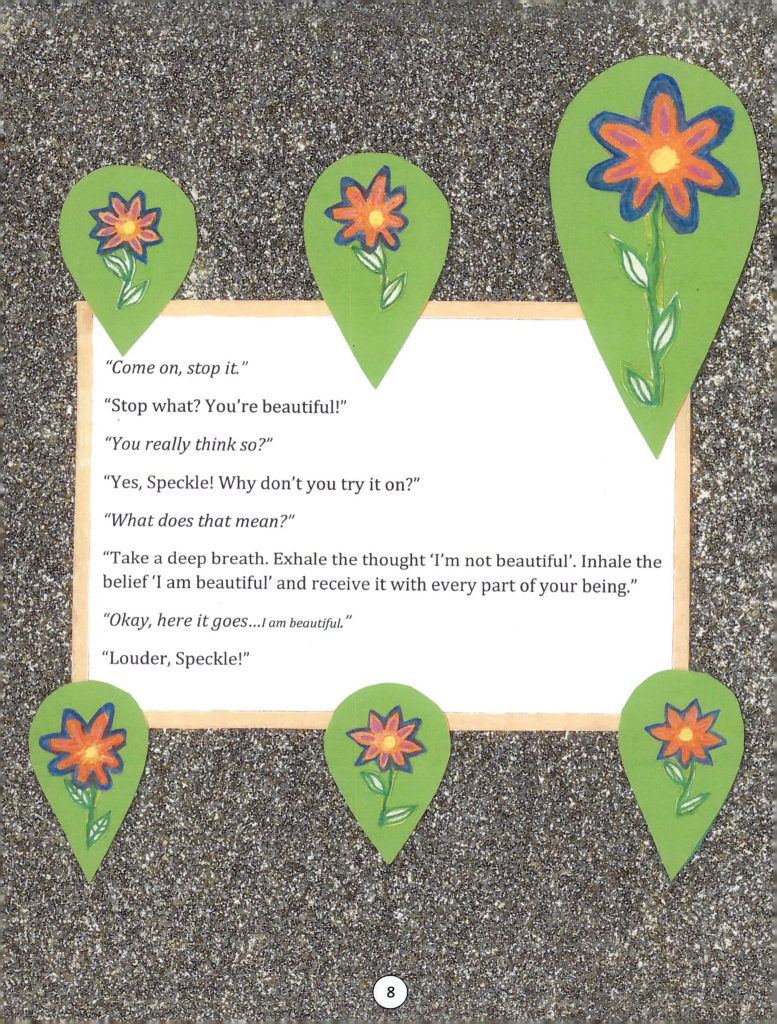

"Come on, stop it."

"Stop what? You're beautiful!"

"You really think so?"

"Yes, Speckle! Why don't you try it on?"

"What does that mean?"

"Take a deep breath. Exhale the thought 'I'm not beautiful'. Inhale the belief 'I am beautiful' and receive it with every part of your being."

"Okay, here it goes...I am beautiful."

"Louder, Speckle!"

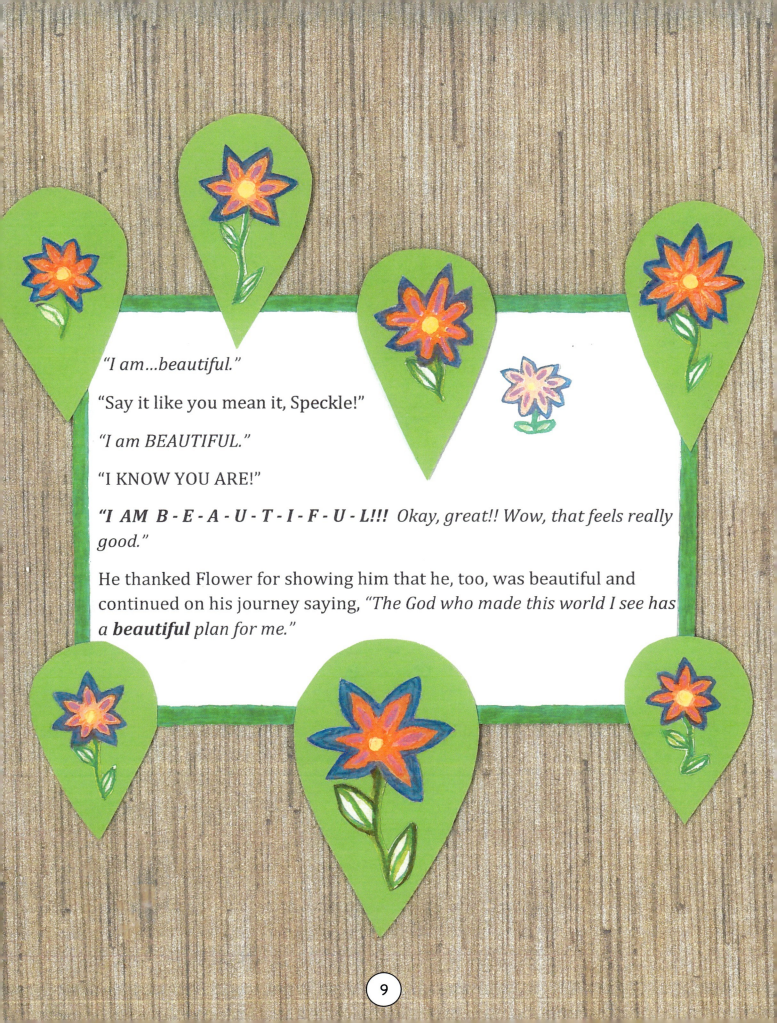

"I am...beautiful."

"Say it like you mean it, Speckle!"

"I am BEAUTIFUL."

"I KNOW YOU ARE!"

***"I AM B - E - A - U - T - I - F - U - L!!!** Okay, great!! Wow, that feels really good."*

He thanked Flower for showing him that he, too, was beautiful and continued on his journey saying, *"The God who made this world I see has a **beautiful** plan for me."*

The next day, Speckle woke up with something warm and bright shining on him. The feeling was wonderful. He stood up and said, *"God? Is that you?"*

A voice responded, "Hi, I'm Sun".

Sun was shining his golden brilliance everywhere.

"Hello Sun, I am searching for the plan God made for me. Do you know anything about it?"

Sun replied:

"God's plan for you is clear and bright.

It activates your inner light."

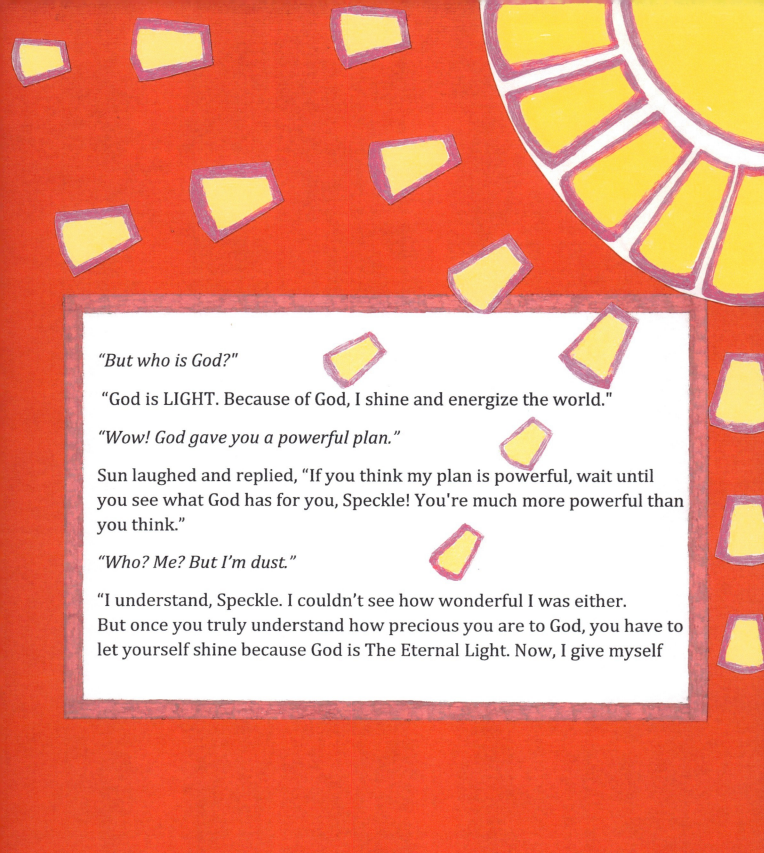

"But who is God?"

"God is LIGHT. Because of God, I shine and energize the world."

"Wow! God gave you a powerful plan."

Sun laughed and replied, "If you think my plan is powerful, wait until you see what God has for you, Speckle! You're much more powerful than you think."

"Who? Me? But I'm dust."

"I understand, Speckle. I couldn't see how wonderful I was either. But once you truly understand how precious you are to God, you have to let yourself shine because God is The Eternal Light. Now, I give myself permission to shine. I accept that I am powerful and I know that you are, too."

"Sun, can you teach me to shine?"

"Sure, I can. Open up and focus on the center of your being. There is a light inside of you, Speckle. It comes from God. What can you tell me about your light?"

"Well, I feel bright when I focus on God's plan for me."

"Good! Imagine that God's plan is living inside of you. It's getting brighter and brighter. Can you see it?"

"Yup, I can see it."

"God's plan is filling you up with light. That light is so powerful that you feel it surrounding you. It fills you up on the inside and you feel it on the outside, too. Do you see the light?"

"Yes, I see the light."

Now, allow yourself to be the light. You are the light and you are living God's plan. Can you feel it?"

"Yes, I can feel it."

"Okay, here is the most important part; Give yourself permission to shine! God smiles when you shine so be as bright as you can be!"

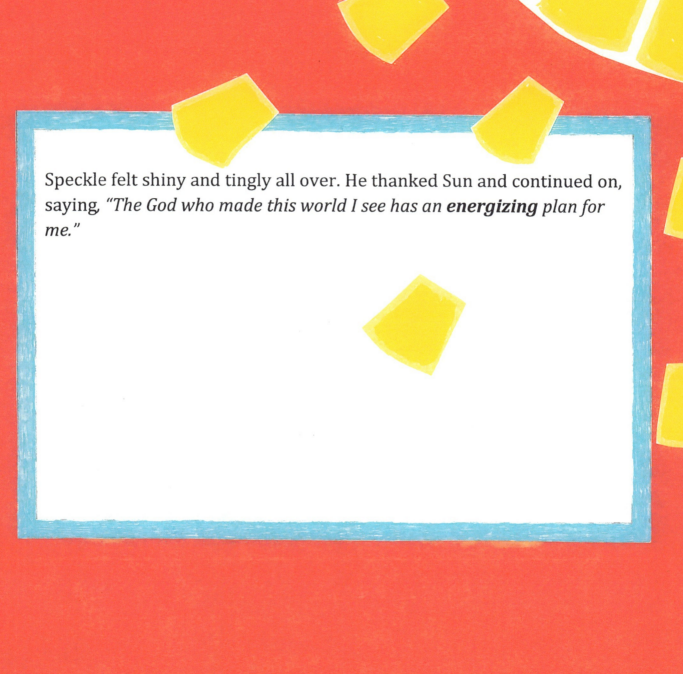

Speckle felt shiny and tingly all over. He thanked Sun and continued on, saying, *"The God who made this world I see has an **energizing** plan for me."*

I give myself permission to shine!

Speckle was unsure about which way to go and it was starting to get late. He noticed there was a soothing, silvery light following him, keeping him company where ever he went.

Suddenly he heard, "Everything is going to be alright, Speckle."

Moon was reassuring him with her glow. Moon was intuitive and could sense what he was feeling. Speckle felt her compassion.

"Moon, do you know God?"

Moon replied, "Yes, God is My COMFORTER and because of God, I have a soothing presence."

"Moon, I am looking for the plan God made for me. Do you know anything about it?"

Moon replied:

"God's heavenly plans for you and me

surpass all of our fantasies."

"Did you just say 'you and me'? But you're Moon. You are high in the sky. How do you know God even sees me?"

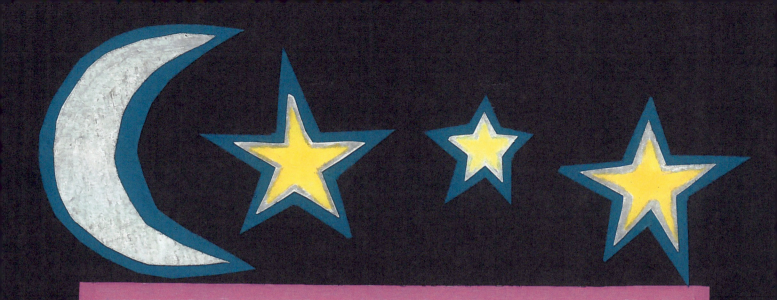

A nearby twinkling Star replied:

"God knows exactly who you are.

He sees your worth from near and far."

Speckle whispered, *"What worth? I'm just dust."*

"Hey, watch it Mister!!" Star warned sternly. "You're one of God's creations and you have tremendous worth. You are divine dust, sacred dust, holy dust, magic dust. Get it?"

Then with compassion in her voice, Star said, "You have to believe in yourself, Speckle. God does."

"What does it mean to believe in yourself?" Speckle asked.

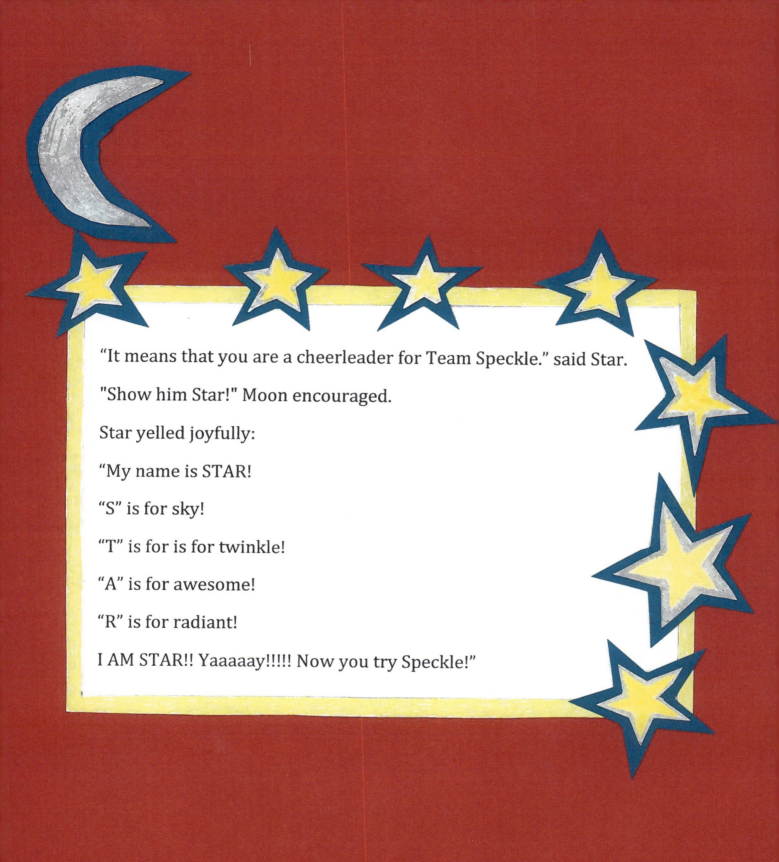

"It means that you are a cheerleader for Team Speckle." said Star.

"Show him Star!" Moon encouraged.

Star yelled joyfully:

"My name is STAR!

"S" is for sky!

"T" is for is for twinkle!

"A" is for awesome!

"R" is for radiant!

I AM STAR!! Yaaaaay!!!!! Now you try Speckle!"

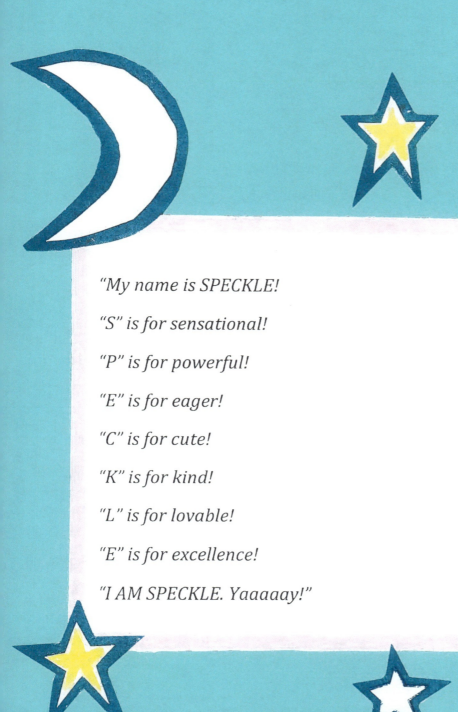
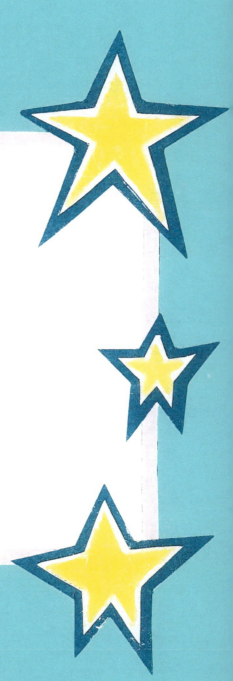

"My name is SPECKLE!

"S" is for sensational!

"P" is for powerful!

"E" is for eager!

"C" is for cute!

"K" is for kind!

"L" is for lovable!

"E" is for excellence!

"I AM SPECKLE. Yaaaaay!"

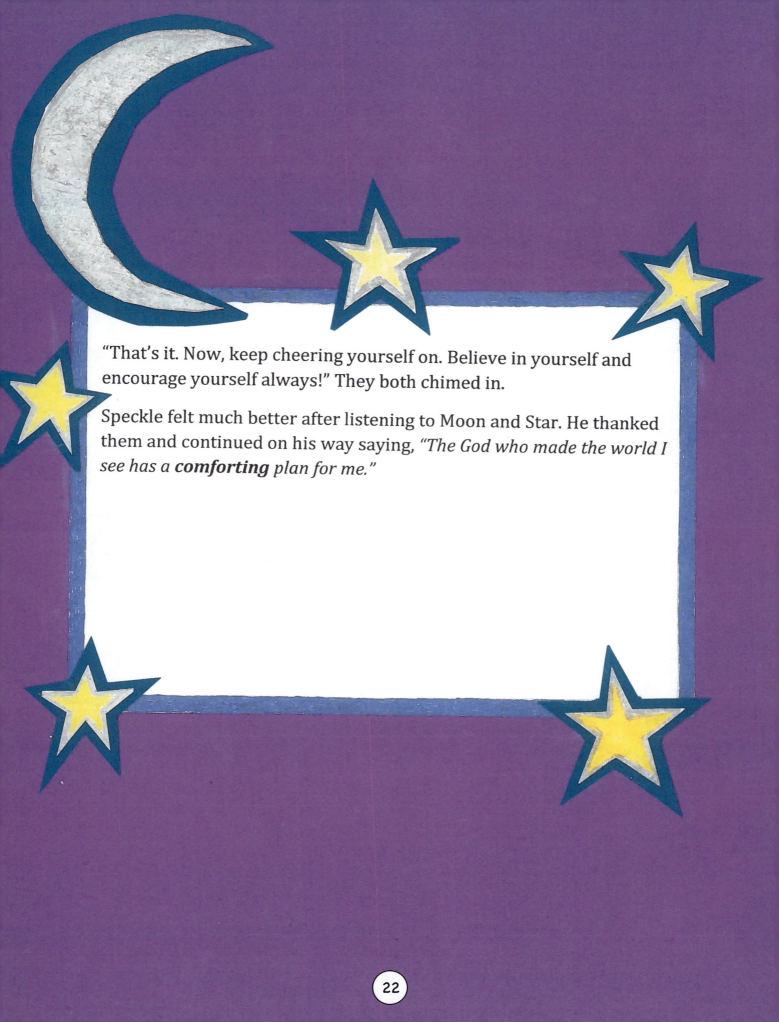

"That's it. Now, keep cheering yourself on. Believe in yourself and encourage yourself always!" They both chimed in.

Speckle felt much better after listening to Moon and Star. He thanked them and continued on his way saying, *"The God who made the world I see has a **comforting** plan for me."*

The next day, Speckle was awoken out of his sleep by a unique sound that he heard in the distance. It was incredibly sweet. So, he decided to follow it.

He found Sparrow singing a beautiful song to her baby chick, soon to hatch out of the egg. Sparrow sang with feeling and her whole body moved with expression to each note.

When she finished, Speckle jumped up, applauding with excitement. He told Sparrow how much he enjoyed her performance and then said, *"Sparrow, I am looking for the plan God made for me. Do you know anything about it?"*

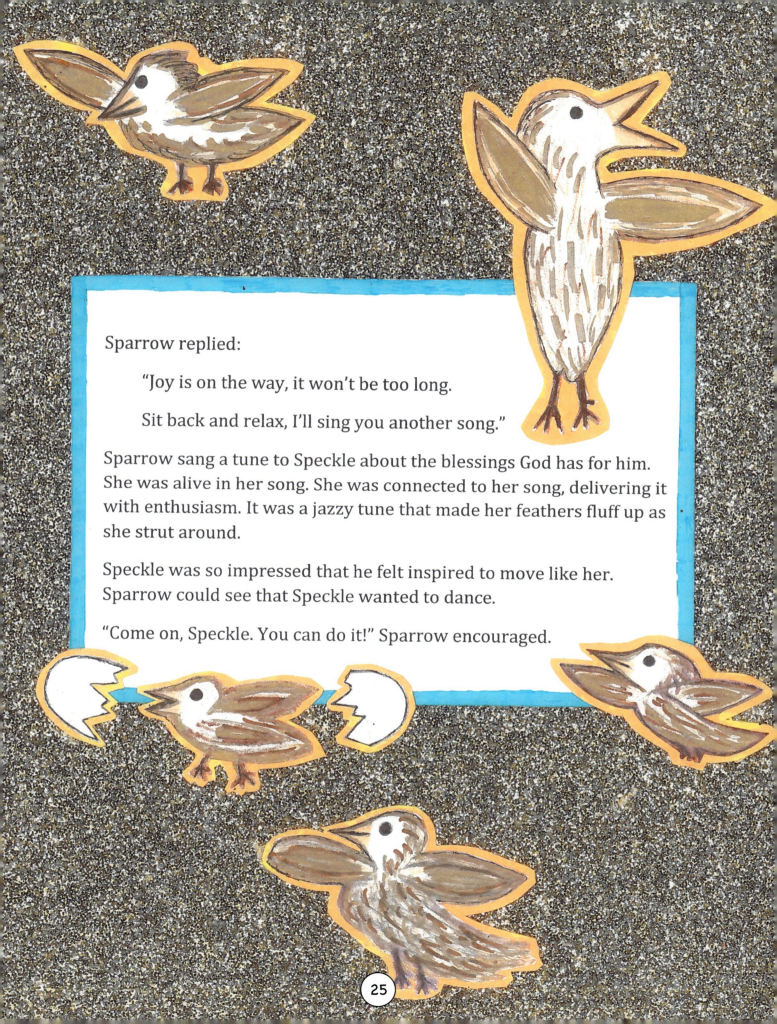

Sparrow replied:

   "Joy is on the way, it won't be too long.

   Sit back and relax, I'll sing you another song."

Sparrow sang a tune to Speckle about the blessings God has for him. She was alive in her song. She was connected to her song, delivering it with enthusiasm. It was a jazzy tune that made her feathers fluff up as she strut around.

Speckle was so impressed that he felt inspired to move like her. Sparrow could see that Speckle wanted to dance.

"Come on, Speckle. You can do it!" Sparrow encouraged.

"But I don't know how to dance."

"Yes, you do! It's already in you. Just let it out. Do what you feel. Listen to the music and listen to your heart. Trust yourself, have fun and move." Then Sparrow pulled him up to show him how.

Speckle followed Sparrow's lead. He jumped, jiggled, and twirled, allowing himself to move freely. When the song was over, Speckle felt totally energized.

"You did it!" Sparrow said.

"I did it!"

"God has wonderful blessings for you, Speckle!"

"But who is God?"

"God is JOY and because of God, I express myself."

"When do I get to live my plan? I'm ready to live my plan now. Maybe I need God's permission first."

Just then, a tiny beak poked through Sparrow's egg. Baby Chick came out saying:

> "You're born because you have a mission.

> And God already gave you permission."

"You know God too, Baby Chick? But you just got here. Who is God to you?" Speckle asked.

"God is LIVING and because of God, I am born."

"That's my baby!!" said Mama Sparrow.

Speckle was most impressed. He thanked Sparrow and Baby Chick, continuing on his journey while saying, *"The God who made this world I see has a **joyful** and **living** plan for me."*

Speckle entered a mountainous area where he noticed Lamb guiding the other sheep through the pasture.

"Good morning, Lamb. I am searching for the plan God made for me. Do you know anything about it?"

Lamb replied:

"Your prayers have been answered, He's heard every word.

Now, receive all your blessings with God as your shepherd."

"What is a prayer?"

"A prayer is your private phone line to God. It's your soul communicating with The Most High. Prayer is a sacred tool and with it, you can create."

"That sounds powerful. Will you teach me to pray?" Speckle asked.

"Yes, let's begin by being quiet and focusing on our hearts."

Then after a few minutes, Lamb asked, "What do you feel in your heart, Speckle?"

"I feel hope and gratitude."

"Why?"

"I hope to find the plan God made for me and I am grateful for all the creations that have supported me along the way."

"Why do you want your plan?"

"Because I feel that I have a purpose and I need to know what it is."

"What else do you feel in your heart?"

"I feel desire. I want to know God. All the creations I have met have such wonderful relationships with God in their own way. I desire to have a relationship with God that fits who I am, too."

"Is there anything else?"

"Yes, I want my plan and my relationship with God to bring me joy and fulfillment."

"Now, take a deep breath, connect with your heart and say all of that to God believing that it is being created for you. Remember to thank God for allowing your prayer to manifest."

Speckle focused on his heart and then said, *"God, I feel hopeful because I believe You have a plan for me. I am grateful for all the creations You have put on my path to support me. I know You have a purpose for me and I thank You for allowing me to find it. Thank You for the wonderful relationship being created between me and You, and for allowing me to live my plan in a way that brings me joy and fulfillment."*

"Now say AMEN."

"AMEN."

Speckle was quiet for a few seconds and then asked, "Who is God?"

"God is MY SHEPHERD, who loves and protects me. He gives me strong leadership qualities so that I properly guide all the other sheep. God wants the best for me and He wants the best for you too, Speckle. You'll see. That was a beautiful prayer. Keep praying."

Speckle continued on his journey thinking about what Lamb had told him; that God listens to his prayers and does love him. He kept going while saying, "The God who made the world I see has a **leading** plan for me."

Speckle soon found himself in grassy plains. He saw Kangaroo in the distance hopping with her Joey. They were both laughing and enjoying each other's company. Speckle noticed how close they were. He could feel the love between them. He longed to know love, also.

Speckle greeted them both and said, *"I am looking for the plan God made for me. Do you know anything about it?"*

Kangaroo smiled and responded:

"You will know God's plan is in its place

when you feel lots of kisses all over your face!"

With that, they started chasing Speckle with hugs and kisses, both sensing that he needed some love. Speckle felt cared for and from his soul, he made a joyful sound. Afterward, Kangaroo responded again to his original question:

"God cares for you in a particular fashion,

with plenty of love and lots of compassion."

"Who is God?"

"God is LOVE and because of God, I feel with my heart and compassion flows inside of me."

"How does love feel?" Speckle asked.

"It's warm and happy. You feel it on the inside." Young Joey replied.

"Joey, do you know God?" Speckle asked.

"Yes. God is AWESOME and because of God, I live in a pouch of love!"

Speckle was aware of a nice feeling on his inside. He thanked Kangaroo and Young Joey for showing him love and then told them that he had to be in his way. They insisted on exchanging hugs with Speckle and nourished him with plenty of affection. He felt himself trust their embrace.

Speckle beamed with love as he continued on his journey while saying, *"The God who made this world I see has a **loving** and **awesome** plan for me."*

The end of the day was approaching and Speckle was trying to come up with a better method for finding God.

"I need to look for God in a bigger way! That's it. I need to cover more territory. I need to…search the universe! But how do I do that?"

"And why would you want to do that?"

"Who said that?" Speckle asked.

"It's me, Universe. I heard you say my name. How is the search going?"

"Well, so far I know that my plan is beautiful, shining, heavenly, joyful, living, shepherding, loving and awesome but I'm still looking for it."

In that moment, Speckle realized that he felt angry and he let it out: *"Where is my plan? Where is God? I want to know God too. Doesn't He want to know me? I looked everywhere I could think to look. Where else am I supposed to go? Don't I matter to God? I WANT MY PLAN AND I WANT IT NOW!!"*

Then he sighed and said, *"The God who made the world I see surely has a plan for me...doesn't He?"*

"Of course God has a plan for you, Speckle."

"Well, how do I find it?"

"God's plan for you will begin

when you choose to look within."

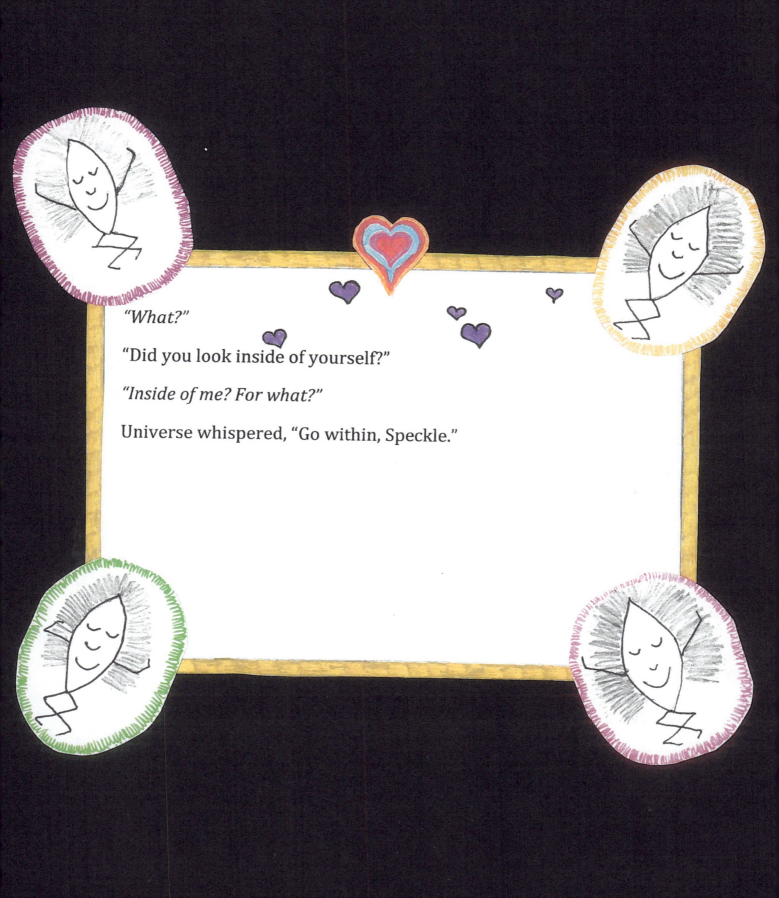

"What?"

"Did you look inside of yourself?"

"Inside of me? For what?"

Universe whispered, "Go within, Speckle."

Speckle stopped looking everywhere on the outside. He was still and quiet. Then he went within to be with himself. It was inside of himself that he found God.

"God?"

"Yes"

"I've been looking for you."

"I've been here, waiting for you to come to me." God said.

"I was told that You have a plan for everything You made. I searched for my plan. I asked every creation I came in contact with about You and they

44

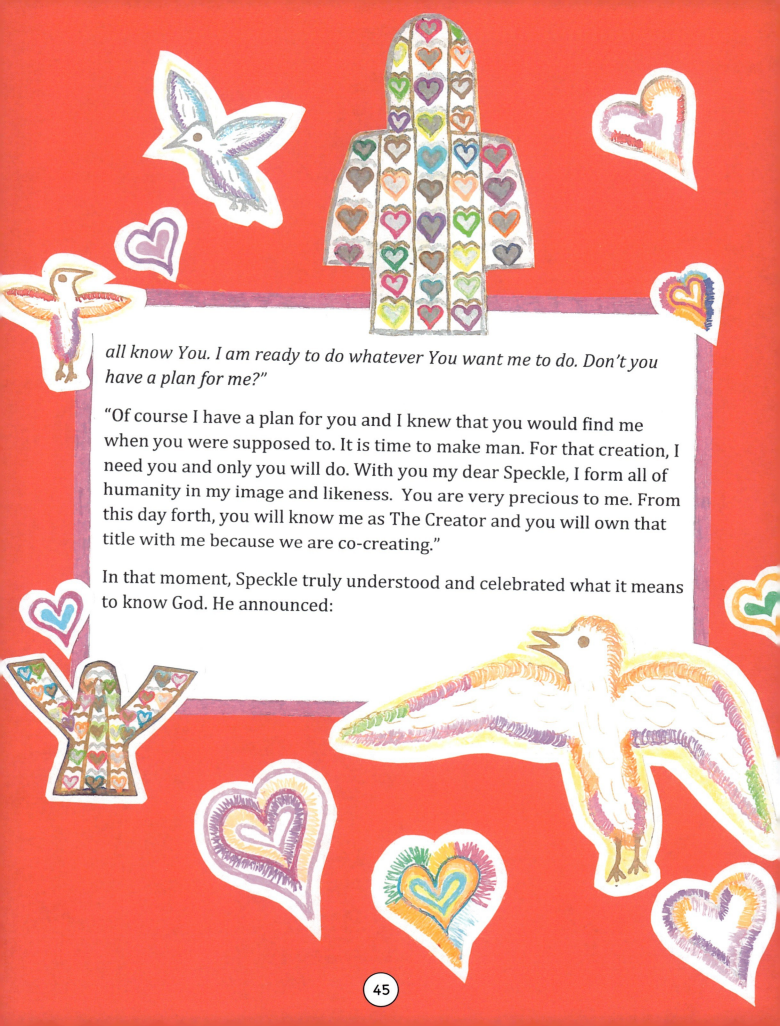

all know You. I am ready to do whatever You want me to do. Don't you have a plan for me?"

"Of course I have a plan for you and I knew that you would find me when you were supposed to. It is time to make man. For that creation, I need you and only you will do. With you my dear Speckle, I form all of humanity in my image and likeness. You are very precious to me. From this day forth, you will know me as The Creator and you will own that title with me because we are co-creating."

In that moment, Speckle truly understood and celebrated what it means to know God. He announced:

"Because of God...

Universe is ETERNAL

Flower is BEAUTIFUL

Sun is LIGHT

Moon and Star are HEAVENLY

Sparrow is JOY

Baby Chick is LIVING

Lamb is LEADING

Kangaroo is LOVE

Kangaroo's Joey is AWESOME

And now, I am CREATING."

Speckle felt a love that was greater than anything he had known before. He transformed into God's favor and sang a new soul song from deep within:

"The God who made the world I see

says we are making man out of... ME!!!!!!!"

"Then The Lord God formed man of the **dust** of the ground and breathed into his nostrils the breath of life." Genesis **2:7**

And They All Lived Happily Ever After

49

I VALUE MYSELF

I ENCOURAGE MYSELF

I ACCEPT MYSELF

I CELEBRATE MYSELF

I CREATE

I FEEL

I RISE

I TRUST

I AM

I PROSPER

I BREATHE

I EXPRESS

I ACHIEVE

I REJUVENATE

I SHINE

Printed in the United States
By Bookmasters